Introduction

We Both Read books can be read alone or with another person. If you are reading the book alone, you can read it like any other book. If you are reading with another person, you can take turns reading aloud. If you are taking turns, the reader with more experience should read the parts marked with a yellow dot ◯. The reader with less experience should read the parts marked with a blue dot ●. As you read, you will notice some difficult words introduced in sections with a yellow dot, then repeated in sections with a blue dot. You can recognize these words by their bold lettering.

Sharing the reading of a book can be a lot of fun, and reading aloud is a great way to improve fluency and expression. If you are reading with someone else, you might also want to take the time, while reading the book, to interact and talk about what is happening in the story. After reading with someone else, you might even want to experience reading the entire book on your own.

Secret of the Old Bones

A We Both Read® Chapter Book

Level 3

Text Copyright © 2017 by D. J. Panec
Illustrations Copyright © 2017 by Brie Spangler
All rights reserved

We Both Read® is a trademark of Treasure Bay, Inc.

Published by
Treasure Bay, Inc.
P. O. Box 119
Novato, CA 94948 USA

Printed in Malaysia

Library of Congress Catalog Card Number: 2016910983

Hardcover ISBN: 978-1-60115-299-2
Paperback ISBN: 978-1-60115-300-5

We Both Read® Books
Patent No. 5,957,693

Visit us online at:
www.WeBothRead.com

PR-11-16

Secret of the Old Bones

By D. J. Panec

Illustrated by Brie Spangler

Contents

TREASURE BAY

Chapter One
A Strange Discovery

"Look!" I called out, coming to a sudden stop.

Aaron, Marcus, and I had biked out to the woods where our town was building a new park and swimming pool. Years ago we had built a treehouse there that we used as a secret hideout. Now as we looked, we saw that a lot of the trees were gone. In their place were about a dozen trucks and bulldozers, all with the name Krud on the side.

"Krud Construction," said Aaron, pointing at a sign. "More like Cruddy Construction if you ask me. They better not have taken down our tree!"

Suddenly we heard someone yelling from up the street. "Hey, Sam!"

I turned to see my cousin Jenny pedaling toward us.

Jenny pulled up in front of us. "Hi, guys! Did Sam tell you I'm staying with his family again this summer? Hope you don't mind me tagging along to see your old clubhouse."

"Clubhouse?" exclaimed Aaron. "This wasn't a clubhouse. This was our hideout. We were fearless pirates back then."

"As I remember it, we were the pirate hunters," said Marcus.

"But we were still pirates," said Aaron. "We were the good pirates fighting the evil pirate bad guys."

Jenny laughed. "The good pirates, huh?"

Meanwhile, I had been wandering around the area. "Hey, I found our hideout," I shouted.

Together we stared at what we once thought was the best place on Earth. Unfortunately, there wasn't much left of it.

"What's this?" said Jenny, pointing to an old sign. "No Girls Aloud. Hmmm. Looks like your work, Aaron."

"Huh? Why me?"

"Aloud?" said Jenny. "Really, Aaron? That's not how you spell *allowed*."

Aaron blushed. "I know that. I was, um, talking about 'loud girls.' No loud girls allowed."

Jenny grinned. "Uh-huh. Sure."

"Hey, Aaron," I said. "Do you remember where you buried your 'treasure'?"

This got Jenny's interest. "Buried treasure?"

Aaron took a small shovel off his bike. "That's right. I buried a box full of very **valuable** things here."

"More like some colorful rocks he found in the creek," I said.

"Some of the rocks could be very rare," said Aaron as he began digging at the base of the tree. "Sometimes something that looks worthless can turn out to be really **valuable**."

After a little digging, he pulled an old metal box out of the ground. We gathered around and looked inside to see an assortment of rocks and stones.

"Well, they are pretty," said Jenny.

Aaron smiled proudly. "Pretty cool, right?"

"Aargh," I said, climbing on my bike. "Now that the treasure be found, let's head back to port, mateys."

"Aye, Captain Sam!" shouted Marcus. "Hoist the sails, ye scurvy crew!"

"How come I'm always the scurvy crew?" grumbled Aaron.

"I'm a bit 'scurvy' meself, matey," said Jenny with a wink.

A few moments later, I stopped my bike at the edge of a huge pit. "Whoa! What is this?"

The others pulled up next to me. "Maybe it's going to be the new swimming pool," Marcus suggested.

"Let's check it out!" called Jenny as she ran into the pit. "Come on!" she called up. "It's not as steep as it looks."

We all made our way to the bottom of the pit, where we found a truck and a mound of something covered with a green tarp. Oddly, the truck didn't have the Krud logo on it anywhere.

Suddenly, Aaron stumbled and fell into the dirt.

"Hey, Aaron," said Marcus. "Tripping over your own feet again?"

"Yes, I'm fine," said Aaron sarcastically. "Thanks for asking." Then he reached over and pulled something from the ground. "Whoa!" he said. "This looks like a bone."

Jenny held up a corner of the green tarp. "Guys! I think there's a whole bunch of bones under here!"

Just then a huge man appeared out of nowhere. "HEY! This area is off limits!" He grabbed Jenny's arm and pointed to a sign. "Can't you read?"

"Let go of her!" I shouted. "She fell into your pit, and we came down to help her."

"I twisted my ankle," Jenny said, starting to limp.

"This area should be fenced," said Marcus. "Someone could get hurt."

The man let go of Jenny. "Yeah, well, that's why it's off limits! Now beat it! And don't come back!"

I helped Jenny limp up a ramp on the other side of the pit.

"And we didn't see your dumb sign," Aaron called back as he and Marcus followed us up.

"That's telling him, Aaron," whispered Marcus with a grin.

Chapter Two
Whose Bones Are These?

"I can't believe that man threatened us like that," said Jenny.

"We were trespassing," Marcus pointed out as he took another sandwich from the stack my mom had prepared for lunch.

Aaron disagreed. "How can it be trespassing if it's a public park?"

"The sign did say the area was **restricted**," I said, "even if we didn't notice it."

"So, what's up with those bones?" Jenny asked. "I think they're hiding something. Literally."

"Maybe it's an old Indian burial ground," I said, "and they know that if someone finds out, they'll have to stop construction."

"Woooo!" moaned Aaron spookily.

"Look, guys," said Marcus. "We're not even sure that they are bones. And even if they are, they're probably just old animal bones."

"So why would they want to hide a bunch of animal bones?" I asked.

"And why was that guard so upset to find us there?" asked Jenny. "Maybe we should tell someone about this. Isn't your dad a policeman, Marcus?"

Marcus nodded. "But what would we tell him? That there might be some bones in a pit in an area marked **restricted**?"

Jenny gave Aaron a teasing grin. "Well, Aaron can't tell his parents. The way he makes things up, they'd never believe him.

"Oh, they'll believe me . . . when I show them THIS!" Aaron dramatically pulled out the bone that he had stumbled over.

Marcus gasped. "Aaron! You stole that bone!"

"I did not steal it!" Aaron cried. "It was on public property."

"It doesn't look like a human bone to me," I said. "Maybe they are just animal bones. I think this calls for a little research."

9

Soon we were all gathered around the clunky old computer my parents let me use.

"How old is this thing, Sam?" Marcus asked, looking at the massive size of the computer.

"Hey, this baby packs a mean punch," I said. "Which is more than I can say about that thing your parents let you use."

"Boys, boys," said Jenny. "Let's focus."

An hour later we had pored through endless images of bones, trying to find one **similar** to the one we had found. But we had no luck.

"Hey," I said, "here's a site that claims it can match any bone to any animal in the world—living or **extinct**."

Jenny began quickly snapping photos of our bone from several angles. "That's perfect! We can upload pics of our bone to the site right now."

In a matter of minutes, the site sent us a report that an exact match for our bone wasn't found. It did, however, appear to be **similar** to the leg bone of a large bird, such as a turkey or an ostrich, or even a bird that was **extinct**.

Marcus threw up his hands. "So someone ate a turkey leg on a picnic, and we have what they left behind."

"A turkey leg?" said Aaron. "If this came from a turkey, it would be the Godzilla of all turkeys!"

"Maybe this isn't a bone at all," I said. "Maybe it's a fossil."

"Isn't a fossil just an old bone?" asked Jenny.

○ "Well, not really," I said. "A bone is made mostly of calcium, so it's almost white in color. And bones are full of tiny spaces, so they're pretty light in weight."

"Right," said Marcus. "But with fossils, minerals have filled in all the spaces of the bone. Over a long time, the minerals harden like a rock. So fossils are usually darker and heavier than bones."

We all noted that our bone was almost brown and seemed pretty heavy for its size.

"There's one other way you can tell sometimes," I said with a smile. "But you have to put your **tongue** on it. If your tongue sticks, it's probably a fossil." I held out the bone and looked around. "Any volunteers?"

"Eww!" said Jenny. "Gross!"

"I'll do it!" said Aaron. He quickly stuck out his **tongue** and touched it to the bone. Then he pulled the bone away from his face and . . . his tongue stuck! He pulled a bit harder, and his tongue came off with a little snap.

"Wow!" said Jenny. "Maybe this is a fossil—from an extinct bird, or even a dinosaur!"

I remembered that the truck in the pit wasn't like the rest of the trucks at the park site and that it didn't have the Krud logo on it. "I wonder if the people at Krud even know about these bones. I mean fossils."

"Well," said Marcus, "why don't we go and ask them?"

Chapter Three
A Visit with Mr. Krud

It was easy enough to find out that Krud **Construction** had its headquarters in an office building downtown and to find out that the head of the company was a Mr. Krud. But it was a little harder to get in to see him.

The woman at the front desk asked if we had an appointment. I told her no, but we really needed to talk to him. "Sorry," she said, but she didn't sound sorry at all.

Just then a man came through the door. He scowled and asked what we were doing there.

"They were just leaving, Mr. Krud," said the woman.

Aaron stepped forward and held up our bone. "Someone is hiding bones at your construction site, sir."

Mr. Krud's eyebrows shot up in surprise. "Oh. Well. Uh, come in then."

We stepped into his office, and I suddenly felt that something wasn't right. I was about to suggest we leave when I noticed a map of the **construction** site on the wall. One area was circled in red and stamped "Restricted." I quietly pointed it out to Jenny.

Meanwhile, Aaron was showing Mr. Krud our bone and telling him about the other bones we'd seen under the tarp—and that they might be valuable fossils.

Mr. Krud laughed in that fake way that adults do when they think you're being silly. "An interesting idea, young man. In fact, it so happens that my workers found those bones last week and we had them checked out. It turns out they're just a bunch of cow bones."

I saw Jenny take out her phone and pretend to be checking for messages, but I noticed that she had turned on the video record function and was actually taking video of the wall map.

Mr. Krud suddenly looked serious. "You know," he said, "you kids should not have been **trespassing** or stealing our property. This may just be an old cow bone, but it's our cow bone."

Krud grabbed for the bone, but Aaron was holding it tight and wouldn't let go.

"Mr. Krud," said Marcus, "we found the bone on public land, so I believe we have just as much right to it as you do."

"Oh, you do, do you?" he sneered.

Just then the same guy we had seen in the pit walked in.

"Is there a problem, Mr. Krud?" he said.

"Bruno, are these the same kids you caught at the construction site?" asked Mr. Krud.

"Yes, they are, sir," Bruno answered.

"Well, they were just leaving. That is, unless they want me to call the police and have them all arrested for **trespassing** and stealing." With that, Mr. Krud jerked the bone out of Aaron's hand and pointed at the door.

Jenny shrugged, pocketed her phone, and led us all out of the room.

Later, we were all having a snack back at my house. Even my mom's chocolate chip cookies weren't cheering up any of us.

"You know," Aaron said, "something is just not right about this. I don't think that Krud guy is telling the truth about the bones being cow bones."

I agreed. "So, let's go over why we think that Krud is **probably** hiding something."

Note to readers: Before I tell you the reasons we came up with, you can take a moment and see if you can think of any reasons that we should have suspected that Mr. Krud might not be telling the truth and that what we found wasn't a cow bone.

"I think," said Jenny, "that if our bone was just a cow bone, that website we used would have said so."

"Also," said Aaron, "the tongue test showed that it's **probably** a fossil. Which means it's really old."

Marcus nodded. "And cows are not native to North America. So an old cow fossil would be pretty much impossible."

"Plus, if Krud really thought it was just a cow bone, why did he want it back so badly?" I added.

Jenny showed the video she shot in Krud's office. She had already marked up the video with some notes. "Look," she said. "He's got the area around the pit marked on his map as restricted. Plus, that guy that chased us off seemed like he was guarding the area. Why would Krud do all that if those were just cow bones?"

"If all this is being done by Krud, why didn't that truck in the pit have a Krud logo on it?" wondered Marcus.

Aaron's eyes narrowed in suspicion. "I'll bet those bones really are valuable fossils and old cruddy Krud is trying to keep them secret."

"Even if the bones are valuable fossils, maybe Krud can claim them for himself since his company found them," said Marcus.

"Hey," I said, "I know someone who knows a lot about fossils."

"Who?" asked Jenny.

"Dr. Mathers," I said. "He works at the Natural History Museum. He talked with my class when we went there for a field trip last year. He's an expert on fossils from this part of the country."

"But we don't have the bone—or fossil, or whatever it is—to show him," Aaron reminded us.

"No worries!" said Jenny, grinning as she took out her phone. "I took pictures of it, remember?"

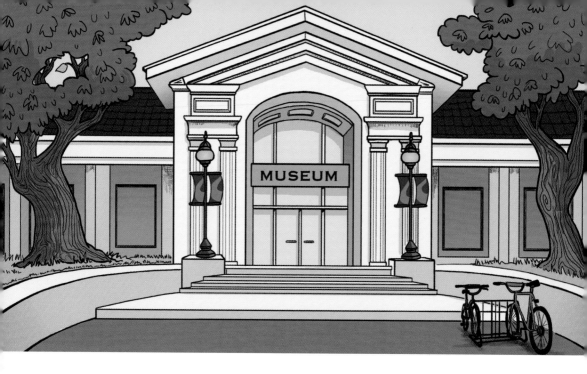

Chapter Four
What's Really Going on Here?

The next day we met with Dr. Mathers at the museum and showed him the pictures.

"Hmm. This does look similar to the leg bone of a large bird," said Dr. Mathers. "But it looks even more like a leg bone from a dinosaur in the raptor family."

Aaron's eyes lit up. "A dinosaur? Cool!"

"What's the raptor family?" asked Jenny.

Dr. Mathers explained that raptors are a certain group of bird-like dinosaurs with three-fingered hands and one sickle-shaped claw on each hind foot. "The group includes Velociraptors and many other bipedal, or two-footed, dinosaurs."

"You think this is a Velociraptor fossil?" I asked.

"Possibly. But there are other types of raptors. It's also possible that these photos could be a hoax."

"They **certainly** are not!" said Jenny. "I took these photos myself."

"May I ask where you got this so-called fossil?"

I quickly explained to Dr. Mathers where we had found it and how Mr. Krud had taken it from us. I asked him if he thought Mr. Krud had the right to keep the fossils if his company had found them. "I mean the fossils are on public land," I said. "So I thought that maybe they should belong to the public."

"You're correct, Sam. Here in the United States, if you find dinosaur fossils in your backyard, you can keep them—or even sell them. But that's not true if you find them on public land, such as a state park."

"So if Krud Construction found dinosaur fossils on city land, they would not belong to Mr. Krud?"

Dr. Mathers shook his head. "No, Sam. They **certainly** would not."

"Dr. Mathers, if this is the leg bone of a **Velociraptor** or some other dinosaur, why does it look so similar to the bone of a large bird?" asked Jenny.

"Excellent question," said Dr. Mathers. "Most scientists now think that modern birds are related to some types of dinosaurs."

"Some dinosaurs," said Aaron. "But not the really cool ones like the T. rex."

Dr. Mathers chuckled. "In fact, Aaron, the Tyrannosaurus rex is thought to be one of the dinosaurs most strongly related to birds. You might even say that birds are modern-day versions of the mighty T. rex!"

Aaron grinned. "So, like when we have chicken for dinner, we're actually eating a modern day T. rex? Well, that's what they get for eating so many humans for breakfast!"

"Aaron, don't be disgusting," said Jenny.

Marcus raised his eyebrows at Aaron. "Uh . . . you do know that dinosaurs and humans never lived at the same time, don't you?"

Dr. Mathers looked down at our photos again. "You know, it's odd that you are showing me these photos today. Before you got here, I was listening to my messages. There was a message from someone named Mr. Durk. He claims to have an almost complete **Velociraptor** skeleton that he is willing to sell to the museum for one million dollars."

"A million dollars?" I exclaimed.

Dr. Mathers said that it was actually a very good price, especially for a full skeleton. Unfortunately, the museum did not have anywhere near that much money for obtaining fossils. "Also, unfortunately, I have a meeting right now, so if you'll pardon me, I must excuse myself."

Dr. Mathers started to leave, but I had one more question. "Dr. Mathers, did this person say where he got the skeleton?"

"Yes, that is also oddly **suspicious**. He said it was discovered on private land here in the United States, which, of course, is not possible." He smiled and turned to go. "I'm sorry, but I really am late."

"Thanks for your help," said Jenny. "I hope we get to see you again."

We all went back to my house to discuss the events of the day and to try to figure out exactly what was going on.

"You know," I said, "that offer Dr. Mathers got to buy a Velociraptor skeleton seems pretty **suspicious**."

"I agree," said Marcus.

Aaron and Jenny shouted out their agreement also.

Note to readers: Before I tell you why we were suspicious, can you think of anything suspicious about the offer of the Velociraptor from Mr. Durk?

"Well," said Jenny, "it's pretty odd that Mr. Durk has a dinosaur skeleton for sale at the same time that Mr. Krud has discovered what are probably dinosaur bones at the park site."

Marcus nodded. "Plus, remember how Dr. Mathers thought it was odd that Mr. Durk claimed to have found his Velociraptor skeleton here in the United States? Did you know that Velociraptors never lived in the United States? They only lived in northern Asia. Other raptor dinosaurs lived here but not Velociraptors. It sounds like Mr. Durk doesn't know a lot about dinosaurs."

"And maybe Mr. Durk doesn't want Dr. Mathers to know where the fossils really came from," I added.

Suddenly Aaron jumped up and shouted, "Hey! Maybe Mr. Durk is Mr. Krud!"

"Why makes you think that?" I asked.

Aaron spelled out the names on a piece of paper. "K-R-U-D. D-U-R-K. See? Durk is Krud spelled backwards!"

"Very impressive, Aaron!" said Jenny. Aaron grinned like he had just won the lottery.

So it seemed that this Mr. Durk didn't know a lot about dinosaurs—or at least not a lot about the one he was trying to sell. We also knew that if Mr. Durk really was Mr. Krud, he didn't have the right to sell the skeleton because it was discovered on public land.

"All that may be true," said Aaron. "But what can we do about it?"

"I think it's time to talk with my dad," said Marcus. "Maybe he'll think it's all suspicious enough to have the police look into it."

Unfortunately, Marcus's dad wasn't very encouraging when we told him our suspicions.

"The idea that Krud and Durk are the same person is an interesting **theory**," he said. "But you have no proof that Mr. Krud has even found dinosaur bones. Jenny's pictures could just be photos of a rubber bone from Halloween. There's no real evidence."

"What if we had an actual bone fossil from the pit?" I asked.

"Well, that might be different." With a warning look he added, "But don't get any ideas. I don't want any of you going anywhere near that pit to get one."

Once he left the room, I said, "Well, if we can't go to the bone, the bone will have to come to us!"

Aaron rubbed his hands together in anticipation. "I think our Sammy boy has an idea."

Chapter Five
A Secret Plan

"Nice to see you again," said Dr. Mathers as he led us into his office.

Jenny quickly explained to him our **theory** that Mr. Durk who was trying to sell him a dinosaur skeleton might really be Mr. Krud.

Dr. Mathers frowned. "Oh dear. I'd hate for such valuable fossils found on public land to be sold to a private collector."

"I think that skeleton belongs right here in this museum," I said.

Dr. Mathers agreed. "But I don't see how that can happen."

"There might be a way," I said, "as long as Mr. Durk thinks you still might want to buy his skeleton."

Together we worked out a plan. Dr. Mathers called Mr. Durk and told him he needed to see the skeleton to verify that it was **genuine** and in good condition. Mr. Durk agreed to bring the skeleton over that evening.

The plan was to have Jenny take some pictures of Mr. Durk without him being aware of it, so we could confirm that Durk and Krud were the same person. Also, Dr. Mathers would ask Durk to leave one of the bones at the museum for a few days so he could run some tests. That way Dr. Mathers could determine the approximate area where it was uncovered. Even if the fossil had been cleaned, there would still be traces of dirt on it to support our theory that it was found in the park area.

Unfortunately, our plan did not go as planned.

That evening, my friends and I hid and watched as a truck pulled up in back of the museum. But the man who got out wasn't Mr. Krud. It was someone we'd never seen before. There went our theory that Krud and Durk were the same person.

Dr. Mathers went inside the truck to look at the fossils. When he came back out, he was holding one of the bones, looking very upset. "Mr. Durk, if those really are **genuine** fossils, they should be packed more carefully!"

"Look," said the man, "I ain't Mr. Durk. Durk is my boss. And he said to tell you that he has another interested buyer. So you've only got one hour to decide."

"What?" exclaimed Dr. Mathers. "I need at least a week to run the tests."

The man grabbed the bone and waved it at Dr. Mathers. "You can have the bone for one hour, Doc. And Durk says it don't leave my sight. Where it goes, I go."

Dr. Mathers sighed. "Well, let's see what we can do in one hour." Then he headed back into the museum with the man at his heels.

"That is definitely NOT Mr. Krud," whispered Jenny.

"No," I said. "But maybe he works for Krud. The truck sure looks like the one we saw down in the pit." I began sneaking toward the back of the truck. "I'm going to get a closer look."

"And I'm going to get my bone back," said Aaron, right behind me.

Marcus hissed, "No, Aaron! That's stealing! Plus, there's another guy sitting in the front of the truck!"

Unfortunately, we didn't hear that last part.

Jenny frowned in concern. "We'd better get that other guy's attention before he hears our boys in the back of the truck." Her frown became a grin as she added, "I think you just broke your leg."

"Huh? What do you mean?" asked Marcus.

As Aaron and I approached the back of the truck, we saw Jenny run toward the front of the truck. She began to pound on the door. "Help! Help! My friend! He's hurt!"

"Hey, kid!" yelled the guy as he opened the door. "Knock it off!"

"My friend needs help!" she said, pointing at Marcus, who was now lying on the ground, clutching his leg. "He fell off his bike. I think he broke his leg."

Meanwhile, I got the back of the truck open and Aaron and I climbed in. Outside, we could hear the guy shouting at Jenny to just call her parents or 911 or something.

Aaron quickly grabbed a fossil in the dark. "I got one," he whispered. "Let's go!"

Then, suddenly, he let out a startled shriek! I turned and almost screamed too as the gigantic skull of what looked like a monster seemed to jump out of the shadows.

The guy outside shouted, "What the heck! Who's in there?"

Our cover was blown.

"Run!" yelled Jenny.

Aaron and I jumped from the back of the truck and raced back to our bikes. We could hear feet pounding the ground behind us, but Aaron and I had a good head start. And Jenny was sprinting way out in front of us.

Chapter Six
Best Day Ever

The next day Marcus's dad came with us to see Dr. Mathers.

"I wasn't able to do much in one hour," said Dr. Mathers, "but I believe the skeleton is probably a Deinonychus (dye-NAW-ni-kus), a dinosaur that lived in this part of North America millions of years ago." He held up the bone that we had taken from the truck. "I'll run more tests on this today."

"I'm sorry," said Marcus's dad, "but there is still no proof that any bones came from Krud's construction site. You'll have to give your bone back to Mr. Durk, Aaron."

"What if we can prove that Mr. Durk is Mr. Krud?" I said.

"Well, then that might be different," said Marcus's dad.

Note to Readers: Can you think of any way to prove that Mr. Durk is Mr. Krud?

I turned to Dr. Mathers. "You said that Mr. Durk left you a voice message. Do you still have it?"

"Yes," said Dr. Mathers.

Then I turned to Jenny. "Jenny, I noticed you recording some video the other day in Mr. Krud's office."

Jenny nodded, beginning to understand where I was going with this. "I was mostly capturing images of his wall map, but voices were being captured as well."

I turned to Marcus's dad. "I think if you run a voice comparison, you'll find a match between Mr. Durk's voice message and Jenny's recording of Mr. Krud."

Marcus's dad smiled approvingly. "Excellent thinking, Sam."

The two voices turned out to be a perfect match, so Marcus's dad let Dr. Mathers run some more tests on the fossil Aaron got from the back of the truck. Traces of dirt on the fossil turned out to be a perfect match with the soil at the construction site, proving it had been taken from public land.

Mystery solved!

We were all pretty disappointed that Marcus's dad wouldn't allow us to be there when Mr. Krud was arrested.

However, we were able to attend the opening of a new exhibit at the museum—an exhibit of the Deinonychus skeleton that we helped to recover.

Dr. Mathers gave a nice speech about the dinosaur and how it had been discovered during construction of the new park. He said that construction at the park was being halted until a team of paleontologists (PAY-lee-uhn-TAW-luh-gists) could complete a search for any other fossils at the site. He also said that when the park opened, it would be named Raptor Park in honor of the dinosaur that was found there.

After his speech, Dr. Mathers made his way over to us. He thanked us again for our help in uncovering the truth about the fossils but wondered why we'd asked him not to mention our names in his speech.

"We talked it over, and we think that it might be better if our identities were kept secret," I said with a sly smile, "just in case there might be any future mysteries that we need to solve."

Marcus's dad groaned. "Please no! I promised all your parents that you would not go snooping around anymore. It's too dangerous."

"We weren't snooping," Jenny pointed out. "We just kind of stumbled on the bones."

"Well, please, no more stumbling," he replied.

Aaron took out his old box of rocks. "Hey, I almost forgot! Dr. Mathers, do you think that I have any valuable rocks or fossils in here?"

Dr. Mathers quickly looked over the contents and concluded that they were all just ordinary rocks.

⸻

"I'm afraid they're only valuable to you," said Dr. Mathers. He paused a moment. "But I do like the old metal box they're in. It looks like it has spent a lot of time in the ground, a bit like our dinosaur here. Would you be willing to loan the box to the museum? I've been thinking of a little exhibit that shows how things that are buried in the ground can change over time."

Aaron's mouth dropped open. "My treasure box? In a museum?" He leaped in the air with a shout. "YES! This is the best day ever!"

I looked at my friends and then over at the Deinonychus. "I agree," I said. "Best day ever!"

41

If you liked *Secret of the Old Bones*,
here is another We Both Read® book you are sure to enjoy!

The Mystery of Pirate's Point

The race is on! It's the annual swim competition
and it looks like the boy's team is going to lose to
the girl's team again! The boys think some girls
stole their mascot, named Lucky. Without their
mascot, the boys are convinced they will never
win. Now, it's up to Sam and his friends to solve
the mystery. If they can find Lucky, maybe they
can also solve the old mystery of Pirate's Point!

To see all the We Both Read books that are available,
just go online to www.WeBothRead.com.